W9-CUE-902

Dear Parents and Educators,

Welcome to Penguin Young Readers! As parents and educators, you know that each child develops at his or her own pace—in terms of speech, critical thinking, and, of course, reading. Penguin Young Readers recognizes this fact. As a result, each Penguin Young Readers book is assigned a traditional easy-to-read level (1–4) as well as a Guided Reading Level (A–P). Both of these systems will help you choose the right book for your child. Please refer to the back of each book for specific leveling information. Penguin Young Readers features esteemed authors and illustrators, stories about favorite characters, fascinating nonfiction, and more!

Oliver and Amanda Oliver, Amanda, and Grandmother Pig	LEVEL **3** GUIDED READING LEVEL **L**

This book is perfect for a **Transitional Reader** who:
• can read multisyllable and compound words;
• can read words with prefixes and suffixes;
• is able to identify story elements (beginning, middle, end, plot, setting, characters, problem, solution); and
• can understand different points of view.

Here are some **activities** you can do during and after reading this book:
• Character Traits: In this book, Oliver and Amanda spend the week with their grandmother. Come up with a list of words to describe Grandmother Pig.
• Summarize: There are five short stories in this book about Oliver, Amanda, and Grandmother Pig. After you read each story, write a short summary of what happened in the beginning, middle, and end of that story.

Remember, sharing the love of reading with a child is the best gift you can give!

—Bonnie Bader, EdM
Penguin Young Readers program

*Penguin Young Readers are leveled by independent reviewers applying the standards developed by Irene Fountas and Gay Su Pinnell in *Matching Books to Readers: Using Leveled Books in Guided Reading*, Heinemann, 1999.

To Grandpa Sam and Grandpa Neil
and Grandma Dorothy—JVL

For Ron—AS

Penguin Young Readers
Published by the Penguin Group
Penguin Group (USA) Inc., 375 Hudson Street, New York, New York 10014, USA
Penguin Group (Canada), 90 Eglinton Avenue East, Suite 700, Toronto, Ontario M4P 2Y3, Canada
(a division of Pearson Penguin Canada Inc.)
Penguin Books Ltd, 80 Strand, London WC2R 0RL, England
Penguin Ireland, 25 St Stephen's Green, Dublin 2, Ireland (a division of Penguin Books Ltd)
Penguin Group (Australia), 707 Collins Street, Melbourne, Victoria 3008, Australia
(a division of Pearson Australia Group Pty Ltd)
Penguin Books India Pvt Ltd, 11 Community Centre, Panchsheel Park, New Delhi—110 017, India
Penguin Group (NZ), 67 Apollo Drive, Rosedale, Auckland 0632, New Zealand
(a division of Pearson New Zealand Ltd)
Penguin Books (South Africa), Rosebank Office Park, 181 Jan Smuts Avenue,
Parktown North 2193, South Africa
Penguin China, B7 Jiaming Center, 27 East Third Ring Road North,
Chaoyang District, Beijing 100020, China

Penguin Books Ltd, Registered Offices: 80 Strand, London WC2R 0RL, England

*The full-color artwork was prepared using carbon pencil, colored pencils, and watercolor washes.
It was then color-separated and reproduced as red, blue, yellow, and black halftones.*

Text copyright © 1987 by Jean Van Leeuwen. Illustrations copyright © 1987 by Ann Schweninger.
All rights reserved. First published in 1987 and 1990 by Dial Books for Young Readers,
an imprint of Penguin Group (USA) Inc. Published in a Puffin Easy-to-Read edition in 1995.
Published in 2013 by Penguin Young Readers, an imprint of Penguin Group (USA) Inc.,
345 Hudson Street, New York, New York 10014. Manufactured in China.

The Library of Congress has cataloged the Dial edition under the following Control Number: 86024326

ISBN 978-0-14-037386-8   10 9 8 7 6 5 4 3 2 1

PENGUIN YOUNG READERS

LEVEL

TRANSITIONAL
READER

3

Oliver, Amanda, and Grandmother Pig

by Jean Van Leeuwen
pictures by Ann Schweninger

Penguin Young Readers
An Imprint of Penguin Group (USA) Inc.

Contents

Chapter 1
The Visit

"Grandmother is coming to visit," said Mother.

"Oh good," said Amanda. "Grandmother and I will read books."

"Grandmother and I will build skyscrapers," said Oliver.

"You can do lots of things with Grandmother," said Mother. "She will be here a whole week."

"Hooray!" said Oliver and Amanda.

Grandmother came after lunch. She unpacked her suitcase. She and

Mother had a cup of tea with honey.

Then she asked, "What shall we do this afternoon?"

"Let's read books," said Amanda.

"Oh dear," said Grandmother.
"I can't find my eyeglasses."

"Then let's build," said Oliver.
"I will get out the blocks."

"Oh dear," said Grandmother.
"I can't sit on the floor. My knees
won't bend anymore. Why don't we
sing songs?"

Amanda climbed onto Grandmother's
lap. So did Oliver.

"You are getting too big to sit on
my lap together," said Grandmother.
"You will have to take turns."

"It's my turn first," said Oliver.

"No, mine," said Amanda.

Oliver pinched Amanda.

Amanda cried. She punched Oliver.

Grandmother covered her ears.

"This is too much noise," she said.

"I am going to take a nap."

Amanda went to find Mother.

"Grandmother is no fun," she said.
"She can't read or sit on the floor.
She thinks we are noisy. And now
she is taking a nap. Grandmother is
too old for naps."

"You are never too old for a nice
nap," said Mother.

"But Grandmother is too old for some things. Like noise and bending over and remembering where she put things. At her house it is always quiet."

"Maybe she should go back to her house," said Oliver. "We can't be quiet for a whole week."

"Try," said Mother.

Oliver and Amanda tried. At dinner they didn't fight or spill their milk.

After dinner Amanda found Grandmother's eyeglasses.

They were on top of the lampshade.

Grandmother read them a
bedtime story.

In the night Amanda had a
dream. It was about monsters.
"Mother!" she called. "Father!"

But no one came. Amanda started to cry.

"It's all right," said Grandmother. "I am here."

She gave Amanda a handkerchief and a big hug.

"Let's sing together," she said.

Amanda and Grandmother sang quiet songs in the dark until Amanda forgot her dream.

"Grandmother," she said. "I am glad you are here."

"Me too," said Grandmother.

Chapter 2
Helping

Amanda woke up early.

Everyone else was sleeping.

She went to the kitchen and

Grandmother was there.

"I always wake up early," said Grandmother.

"Me too," said Amanda. "And I feel lonely."

"Let's have breakfast together," said Grandmother.

Amanda set the table.

"I can't reach the cups," she said. "They are up too high."

"I will help you," said Grandmother.

Grandmother cooked.

"I can't reach the pots," she said. "They are down too low."

"I will help you," said Amanda.

They ate breakfast.

Still everyone else was sleeping.

"Let's go to the mailbox," said Amanda.

Grandmother and Amanda walked down the road.

It was hard for Amanda to walk so slowly.

"Look," said Grandmother. "Flowers."

"Let's pick some," said Amanda.

"I can't," said Grandmother.

"I will help you," said Amanda.

Grandmother helped Amanda
reach the mailbox.

Amanda helped Grandmother
carry the mail.

They put the mail and the flowers
on the kitchen table.

Still everyone else was sleeping.

"Let's read books," said Amanda.

"Good idea," said Grandmother.

"I can't read by myself," said Amanda. "I don't know the words yet."

"I have trouble reading by myself, too," said Grandmother. "I can never find my eyeglasses."

Amanda found Grandmother's eyeglasses. This time they were under her pillow.

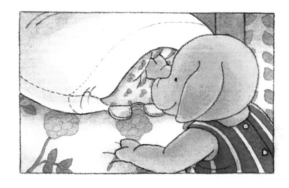

"It's good we have each other,"
said Grandmother.

They read four books, and then
Father got up.

"Good morning, early birds,"
he said.

"Grandmother and I have had breakfast," said Amanda. "And we got the mail and picked flowers and read four books."

"You did all of that already?" said Father.

"Yes," said Amanda. "I helped Grandmother, and Grandmother helped me."

"That is nice," said Father.

"Grandmother," said Amanda. "Can we be early birds again tomorrow?"

"I will meet you in the kitchen," said Grandmother, "at seven o'clock."

Chapter 3
Bad Oliver

"Oh dear," said Grandmother. "I have lost my eyeglasses again. I have looked everywhere."

"Look in the mirror," said Oliver. "You are wearing them."

"Why, so I am!" said Grandmother. Oliver and Amanda laughed.

"Grandmother is so silly," said Oliver. "I am going to play a trick on her. I am going to hide her eyeglasses."

"You better not," said Amanda. "You will get in trouble."

"No, I won't," said Oliver.

While Grandmother drank a cup of tea, Oliver took her eyeglasses. He put them on his tiger.

"Grandmother will never find her eyeglasses this time," he said.

"Has anyone seen my eyeglasses?" asked Grandmother.

"I bet Oliver can find them," said Amanda.

"No, I can't," said Oliver.

Everyone looked but no one could find them.

"What will I do?" said Grandmother.
"I can't see without my eyeglasses."

"Oliver," said Amanda. "Are you sure you can't find them?"

Everyone looked at Oliver.

He went to his room and got his tiger.

"Here they are!" he said.

"Oliver," said Father. "That was a bad thing to do. Go to your room and stay there."

"It was only a trick," said Oliver.

"Go!" said Father.

Oliver sat in his room all alone.
He could hear everyone talking. He
could smell dinner cooking. But no
one called him to have some.

There was a knock on the door.

It was Grandmother.

She sat down next to Oliver on his bed.

"When I was little," she said, "I once did something very bad."

"As bad as me?" Oliver asked.

"Worse," said Grandmother.

"My mother always used to sit in her rocking chair and sew. One day I took a pincushion and put it on her chair."

"What happened?" asked Oliver.

"Well," said Grandmother. "She sat down, and then she screamed and got up again very fast."

Oliver laughed.

"Was your mother angry?" he asked.

"I was sent to my room without any dinner," said Grandmother.

"Just like me," said Oliver. "Bad Grandmother."

"I never did it again, though," said Grandmother.

"I will never hide your eyeglasses again," said Oliver.

"Good," said Grandmother. "I think there might be some dinner waiting for you downstairs."

"Would you sit with me while I eat it?" asked Oliver.

"I would," said Grandmother.

Chapter 4
Thunder and Lightning

"Good-bye," said Mother. "I am going to the store."

"Who will take care of us?" asked Amanda.

"Grandmother," said Mother. "You know she always took care of me when I was little."

"But maybe she has forgotten how to do it," said Oliver.

"There are some things you never forget how to do," said Mother.

Oliver and Amanda played outside.

"Look at the sky," said Amanda.
"It's nighttime already."

"It can't be," said Oliver. "We just
had lunch."

"Oliver! Amanda!" called
Grandmother. "Come inside. It is
going to rain."

Amanda put away her wagon.

"What was that noise?" she asked.

"Thunder," said Grandmother.

"I'm scared of thunder," said Amanda. "It sounds like a monster growling."

"I don't like lightning," said Oliver.

"Come," said Grandmother. "I will tell you a story."

"About when you were little?"
asked Oliver.

"Yes," said Grandmother.

She told them a funny story
about going on a picnic with her six
sisters and five brothers.

"Grandmother," said Amanda. "The thunder is getting louder."

"If we sing songs," said Grandmother, "maybe we won't hear it."

They sang loud songs. Oliver beat on his drum. But they could still hear thunder and rain beating on the roof.

"I'm scared," said Amanda. "I want this storm to stop right now."

"It won't stop until it's over," said Grandmother. "But I know how we can stop listening to it. We will need a lot of pillows."

Oliver and Amanda got pillows from their rooms and pillows from the couch.

"More than that," said Grandmother. They got pillows from Mother and Father's room and pillows from the big chair.

"That may be enough," said Grandmother. "Now cover your ears with pillows."

Oliver put two pillows on each ear.

Amanda covered herself with pillows.

"I can't hear a thing," she said.

She couldn't breathe, either. She took one off.

"Hey, watch out," said Oliver.

He threw the pillow at her.

Amanda threw it back.

It hit Grandmother.

"Pillow fight!" said Oliver.

Grandmother and Oliver and
Amanda laughed and threw pillows
until they were all tired out.

"Listen," said Grandmother.

Outside everything was quiet.

"The storm is over," said Amanda.

"That was a bad storm," said

Oliver. "But you took care of us. You

didn't forget how."

"There are some things you

never forget how to do," said

Grandmother.

Chapter 5
Good-Bye

Grandmother was packing up.
Tomorrow she was going home.

Amanda helped Grandmother.
She reached things for her and
carried things for her and sat on her
suitcase to close it.

"That was hard work," said
Grandmother. "I need a nap before
dinner."

Amanda went to the kitchen. Mother
was cooking.

"What are you making?" she asked.

"A good-bye dinner for
Grandmother," said Mother.

"It has all of her favorites: liver and onions and lima beans."

"Liver?" said Oliver. "Lima beans? Grandmother's favorites are not my favorites."

"Can we make something for Grandmother, too?" asked Amanda.

"What would it be?" asked Mother.

"A good-bye cake," said Amanda. "It will be all pink."

"I like chocolate cake," said Oliver.

"Why don't you make a chocolate and pink cake?" said Mother.

Oliver and Amanda mixed up the cake.

Mother baked it. On top they wrote with icing: GOOD-BYE.

When Grandmother got up from her nap, she said, "Something smells good."

"It is your good-bye dinner," said Oliver.

Grandmother liked her good-bye dinner. Oliver and Amanda didn't.

Except for the cake.

"We made it ourselves," said Amanda.

"Look what it says on top," said Oliver.

"Oh dear," said Grandmother. "Where have my eyeglasses gone?"

"I will find them," said Amanda. She looked all over.

"You won't believe it," she said. "They were in the wastebasket."

"I will miss having you to find my eyeglasses," said Grandmother.

"I will miss being early birds together," said Amanda.

"I will miss hearing stories about when you were little," said Oliver.

"And singing songs," said Amanda.

"Do you know what I will miss the most?" said Grandmother.

"What?" asked Oliver.

"Your noise," said Grandmother. "It is too quiet at my house."

"Soon we will come to visit you," said Oliver. "And we will make lots of noise."

"Oh good," said Grandmother.

"Now who would like a slice of cake?

"Me!" said Oliver and Amanda.

And they all had big slices of

Grandmother's good-bye cake.